POKÉMON™
THE SERIES
SUN & MOON

Old Buddies, New Battles

Adapted by Jeanette Lane

Scholastic Inc.

CHAPTER 1

Now, class!" Principal Oak's dark eyes sparkled with excitement. He waited for all the students to pay attention before he continued. "To celebrate the twentieth anniversary of our beloved Pokémon School, we're going on an extra-special field trip."

"Special field trip?!" said Ash Ketchum.

Ash could hardly believe his luck. First of all, he was living in the gorgeous, tropical Alola region and attending the famous Pokémon School. Now that he'd been there for a few months, he felt like a real student, and he claimed all his classmates as friends.

The Pokémon School was like no other. It was a place where people and Pokémon learned together. He and Pikachu fit right in! Principal

Oak and Professor Kukui had taught them many new things, especially about the unique Pokémon of the Alola region.

For Ash, the only thing better than going to the Pokémon School was going on a Pokémon School field trip! Ash couldn't wait to hear where they were headed.

"So does that mean we get to go to some amazing place?" Mallow wondered.

Ash, Mallow, Sophocles, Lana, Kiawe, and Lillie all leaned forward with anticipation.

"We sure do," Professor Kukui answered. He paused before declaring, "We are going to the Kanto region!"

"Oh, boy," Ash mumbled. "Kanto, huh?"

For Ash, Kanto did not seem extra-special or amazing. After all, Kanto was his home region. He had hoped to travel somewhere new. He wanted to learn more about regional differences of Pokémon, or meet famous Pokémon Trainers.

"You're from the Kanto region, aren't you, Ash?" Kiawe asked. He studied Ash with a serious gaze that was typical Kiawe.

"Yeah," Ash replied, still bummed.

The others didn't feel that way at all. "Professor Oak's world-famous laboratory is there, right?" Sophocles asked, sounding excited.

"Yes, indeed!" Principal Oak declared. "We'll visit my cousin Professor Oak at his laboratory, plus you'll get to see lots of Kanto Pokémon, too!"

"Right, and that's not all," Professor Kukui added. "I want you to be able to *Tackle* an experience you can't have here, along with some very special guests."

"Special guests? Who are they?" Now Ash was curious. Who were the guests? Did he know them?

"And just what *can't* we do in Alola?" Mallow wondered, twisting one of her long green pigtails. She was adventurous and loved new experiences.

"You'll have to wait to find out until we get there," Professor Kukui said, sounding mysterious.

"Sounds like lots of fun!" Kiawe and Sophocles said at the same time.

"Sure does!" agreed Lana, Lillie, and Mallow.

Soon, the whole crew was on its way. Once they were on the plane, Ash had totally come around. He was going to get to visit home! He'd get to see his mom!

"Man, I can't wait to get there," Ash said, his own excitement growing. "I'll be able to show you guys around." He thought of all the things he'd like to share with his new friends.

"That'll be perfect!" Mallow agreed.

Although returning to the Kanto region wasn't new for Ash, the trip would provide new experiences for his classmates—some more than others.

"Hey, Sophocles! How is this thing flying?!" Kiawe asked nervously as he peered out the airplane window. He took a deep breath in and out, fogging up the glass. It was unusual to see the normally composed and brave Kiawe, proud owner of a Z-Ring, seem so anxious.

Sophocles showed no signs of fear. "As far as I'm concerned," he replied, "it's a whole lot safer than a Charizard."

It was clear Kiawe would much prefer to be riding his trusted fire-breathing Pokémon than be trapped inside a machine with metal wings and roaring engines.

Despite Kiawe's concerns, they all landed at the Kanto airport safe and sound. "Here we are!" Ash announced, already seeing familiar sights as they walked through the airport.

"Hope we get to see a Vileplume!" Mallow said.

"Horsea and Seadra, too!" Lana added, focusing on her favorite—Water-type Pokémon.

Everyone was looking forward to the coming adventure—except Lillie.

"Oh no. Is something wrong, Snowy?" Lillie asked, leaning over her beloved Pokémon. She could tell something wasn't right. Her Alolan Vulpix looked tired and droopy. Even its tail looked less fluffy. "Don't you feel well? Poor dear . . ." Snowy collapsed in her arms. "Now what should I do?"

Lillie was a worrier by nature. Even though she had read hundreds of books about Pokémon over the years, she was not sure how to handle certain situations. And they were in a new, foreign place. What was Lillie going to do?

CHAPTER 2

Lillie looked around. The rest of the Pokémon School group had moved ahead. Lillie rubbed Snowy's soft head and mumbled to herself. She wasn't sure what to do.

"Excuse me," said a stranger with a low voice and a thick crop of dark hair. "Your Vulpix, would you mind if I examine it?" He carried a medical bag. "See, I'm actually studying to become a Pokémon doctor."

Lillie let out a sigh of relief. "That would be great! We got off the plane, when all of a sudden . . ." Lillie's voice faltered with concern.

"Leave it to me." The stranger seemed very steady, and he looked trustworthy in his vest with many pockets. He carefully examined Snowy, who let out weak moans now and again.

Of course, Lillie had no way of knowing that the stranger was not a stranger to Ash at all. It was his old friend and traveling companion, Brock!

Meanwhile, some other familiar faces had also recently arrived from Alola. They were not exactly strangers, but they weren't friends either. Team Rocket was in the Kanto airport, and they were all in foul moods, as always.

"Ugh, this is so depressing," Jessie complained.

"Going through all of this to get to headquarters," James continued. They were annoyed.

"So why do we have to take orders from that gal with the bob haircut and wire-rimmed glasses, anyway?!" Meowth wondered out loud.

Jessie, James, and Meowth were frustrated with the fact that their boss had someone new working for him. What was even worse was that the new person seemed to think the members of Team Rocket worked for her. Jessie, James, and Meowth despised her attitude.

"If we don't follow her orders, we'll get more lectures than in all my school years combined!" James whined.

"Hey, no sweat," Meowth said. "If we give Loser Locks this yummy pastry, she's sure to get in a good mood!" Meowth held up a sticky bun in hopes that it would be a good bribe, but then he frowned. "Yeah, like that's gonna work."

The airport was so crowded, no one from the Pokémon School noticed Jessie, James, and Meowth.

Lillie, especially, did not notice them. She was too focused on Snowy.

"Just as I suspected," Brock said. "A little airsickness." He put the stethoscope back in his medical kit.

"Oh, thank you very much!" Lillie said, snuggling with her Vulpix.

"I wonder what's keeping Lillie," Mallow said to Ash.

Ash glanced around. He spotted Lillie, and then he noticed she was talking to someone. Ash would recognize that figure anywhere!

"Is that Brock?!" he wondered out loud. "Heyyyy! Brock!" he yelled, racing straight for his old friend.

Brock looked up, but he didn't seem to notice Ash. He'd spotted a young flight attendant. "Wow!" He ran right past Ash and stopped in front of the young woman. "Ahh . . . wouldn't it be paradise if we flew the lovely skies together!"

Brock was infamous for falling in love fast. He began one of his trademark love poems, pulling a bouquet of roses out of nowhere and presenting them to the flight attendant. "Chasing clouds with you . . . Soaring on love's wing . . ."

Brock sounded very devoted—until someone started to yank his earlobe. "Ow, ow, ow, ow, ow . . . OW!" he yelped.

"Really? I come all the way to pick you up at the airport, and *this* is the thanks I get?!" said the person pulling on Brock's ear.

"Ha! Misty!" Ash could hardly believe it. It was his old friend Misty pinching Brock's ear! Ash's two original traveling companions were right here in the airport.

"Hey, Ash!" Misty said with a friendly wave. She wore the same jean shorts; red suspenders; and cute, lopsided ponytail as always. "How have you been doing?"

Pikachu was so excited, it bounded right off Ash's shoulder and into Misty's arms.

Releasing her hold on Brock's earlobe, Misty gave Pikachu a genuine hug. "Long time no see, Pikachu!" she greeted the affectionate Pokémon with a giggle.

From behind a nearby pillar, Team Rocket watched the reunion of their longtime enemies. "It's the original Twerp, Twerp, and Twerpette trio!" Jessie moaned.

"What are they doing here?" James asked,
his eyes narrowed.

"Let me introduce you," Ash said, turning to
his Pokémon School classmates. "These are my
friends, and we traveled together before."

"Nice to meet you. I'm Misty, internationally
known beauty," said Misty. "I'm also the
Cerulean City Gym Leader!"

"You're a Gym Leader?" Mallow's voice was
full of admiration.

"And an . . . internationally known beauty?" Lana asked.

"I'm Brock! A Pokémon Breeder as well as a Pokémon doctor in training. I'm also the former Pewter City Gym Leader," he explained. "The pleasure to meet you is mine, all mine."

"Hi there, Brock. My name's Sophocles!" Sophocles, like many of the students, held his favorite Pokémon in his arms. Togedemaru chirped a hello as well.

"I'm Lillie."

"I'm Kiawe."

"My name's Mallow!"

"And I'm Lana." From its perch on Lana's head, Popplio waved a friendly fin.

"What are you two doing here?" Ash asked, looking from Misty to Brock.

"Well, Professor Oak asked us to come," Misty admitted.

Ash nodded. "So you must be the special guests!"

"Hold on!" Professor Kukui called out. "We'll get to the truth and quash any rumors when we're on the road!"

"Right, my cousin is waiting. *Shellos* we go?" Principal Oak said. He loved using Pokémon names as puns.

Team Rocket had been just close enough to eavesdrop on the whole conversation. "Sounds like they're on their way to Professor Oak's lab," Jessie pointed out with a scowl.

"That crib is the picture-perfect place to pick a pile of primo Pokémon!" Meowth proclaimed.

The Normal-type Pokémon was always thinking ahead.

"I predict if we catch them all and present those Pokémon to the boss, it will be lecture over and class dismissed!" Jessie said, hatching a plan to get back on the boss's good side.

"Wobbuffet!" Wobbuffet, an often-silent member of Team Rocket, announced its approval.

Jessie was right. If Team Rocket could infiltrate the grounds of Professor Oak's lab, they might be able to steal some of the best-trained and most powerful Pokémon of all time—Pikachu, Turtonator, Popplio, Steenee, Togedemaru, and so many more.

But would Team Rocket's plan to steal all the Pokémon School students' best battle partners actually work?

CHAPTER 3

After a short ride past rolling meadows, tall forests, and clear rivers, the crew arrived at Professor Oak's famous Pokémon laboratory. With its plum-colored roof and tall windmill, it made quite a landmark. While Ash had been there many times before, his classmates were in awe.

"Samson!" Professor Oak called out as everyone entered the laboratory.

"Dear Samuel!" Principal Oak returned the greeting, grabbing his cousin's hand and giving it a firm, friendly shake.

"Congratulations on the twentieth anniversary of your Pokémon School!" Professor Oak said.

"Thanks, cousin!"

"They're the same!" Rotom Dex cried out. It hovered between the two cousins, calculating each one's appearance. "Except for their hair, their other features—like their noses and mouths—are a 99.9 percent match!"

It was true! Principal Oak had long gray hair and wore a short-sleeved tropical shirt. The professor had shorter, light-brown hair and wore a buttoned shirt and white lab coat, but the two men still looked very much alike.

"Everyone! This is my dear cousin and the world's leading authority on Pokémon research," the principal announced to his students. "Let me present Professor Samuel Oak!"

"Ahem." Professor Oak cleared his throat. "And now I believe it is time for a Pokémon poem." He paused before reciting his lines.

Twenty years.
How Bulbizarre *the passing of time can be,*
Catching Pokémon for everyone to see!

The principal, Professor Kukui, and the Pokémon School students all clapped. Even Popplio flapped its fins together.

"Here's one of my poems for you!" Rotom Dex said. It went up to Principal Oak and Professor Oak and recited its poem right next to the cousins.

Same faces,
side by side.
A Bulbizarre *ride!*

"Brilliantly done!" Principal Oak and Professor Oak announced in unison.

"Poetry's fun!" Rotom agreed.

Next, Professor Oak invited everyone to take a long tour of the Pokémon laboratory grounds. "I've asked Brock and Misty to be your guides," he said. "I know they'll be great!"

"Thanks!" Brock replied.

"We won't let you down!" Misty assured them.

"Whoa," Mallow and Kiawe said together as they stepped outside through double doors.

"It's huge!" Sophocles observed as he took in the lush green fields, tree-covered hills, and vast blue sky. There was a fenced-in area, a large barn, and lots of space for Pokémon to roam free.

"And so many Pokémon, too!" said Lillie. She could see such a variety of Pokémon milling around the grounds, including Exeggcute, Bellsprout, Chansey, and more.

"Yeah, right?" Ash agreed.

"Some of these Pokémon have Trainers who asked us to care for them while they're gone," Brock told the group. "Some are Pokémon we've taken in. And some are wild Pokémon who just showed up."

"No time to waste, so let's go see them!" Misty said.

"This is the perfect place to gather Pokémon data!" Rotom Dex was in heaven! It had so much new data to collect on Kanto Pokémon.

Sophocles glanced around. "I want to see a Kanto Raichu!" he said.

"When I think of Kanto," Kiawe said, "it's got to be Fire-type Pokémon." Kiawe had no problem admitting he had a favorite type.

Lana repeated her own wishes for Kanto sightings. "Horsea! Seadra!"

"There are so many Pokémon I want to see . . ." said Lillie. "Oh, look! Ooh, a Spearow!"

"We have them in Alola, too," Mallow pointed out.

"I guess you're right," Lillie admitted with an
embarrassed grin. She just adored all
Pokémon.

"A lot of my Pokémon are living here, too,"
Ash said. "There they are!" He pointed across a
long flat field to a herd of large Wild Bull
Pokémon. "Hey! Look, Tauros, it's me!"

At once, the Pokémon stopped grazing and
looked in the direction of the small school
group. Ash rushed out, excited to be reunited
with his Pokémon. But the whole herd began to

stampede toward him, hooves pounding the ground.

Ash didn't look very concerned, but his friends were!

"What's going on?!" Mallow cried, her hands held up to her face in shock.

"What's Ash doing?!" Sophocles said, stating the question they were all wondering.

"Tauros!" Ash yelled as they grew near, but the Wild Bull Pokémon were going too fast to slow down. Even Pikachu grew alarmed as one of the Tauros hit Ash head-on, and the young Pokémon Trainer was tossed high into the sky.

Luckily, Ash wasn't hurt, but that was the last time he'd ever yell to a whole herd of Pokémon with moves like Zen Headbutt, Horn Attack, and Giga Impact!

There was so much to see in Kanto! It was hard to stay together because everyone wanted to investigate different new and exciting Pokémon.

Kiawe wandered away from the group, taking in the beautiful surroundings. He came to a grassy ridge and noticed a majestic Pokémon standing at the top.

"Wow! That's—"

"Rapidash," Rotom Dex finished Kiawe's sentence. "The Fire Horse Pokémon. A Fire-type. Rapidash loves to gallop. Whenever it sees something moving fast, it gets the urge to race."

Kiawe knew another Pokémon who loved to race! He watched Rapidash run down a dirt bank to a grassy field. The Fire Horse Pokémon looked so at ease as it galloped. It grew faster with each stride, its mane and tail streaming behind it like a wild flame.

Kiawe was amazed. "All right! Charizard, let's go!" he yelled. He tossed a Poké Ball, and his own Flame Pokémon appeared.

"Ready to fly?" Kiawe asked.

Charizard took off with a mighty flap of its wings. Soon, the Pokémon and Trainer were soaring right behind the Fire Horse Pokémon. "Want to have a race, Rapidash?"

With a giddy snort, Rapidash accepted the challenge. It burst ahead with new speed.

Charizard soared just above the galloping Pokémon. They kept pace with each other. Rapidash threw its head in the air and whinnied to Kiawe.

"Really?" Kiawe asked. "You want me to hop on?"

Carefully, Kiawe leaned over Charizard's side and landed on Rapidash's back. Almost immediately, he yelped. The Pokémon's mane was on fire!

"I'm in awe!" he said, thrilled.

"Kiawe! How far are you going?" Rotom Dex called out. There was concern in its voice, but Kiawe didn't even look back.

Not far away, the other Pokémon School students were encountering more Pokémon from the Kanto region.

"So this is a Vileplume for real!" Mallow declared. "And a pair of Gloom, too! *Alola*, cuties!" She leaned over to get a closer look at the colorful Flower Pokémon and the Weed Pokémon.

"Vileplume's pollen is poisonous!" Brock warned from a distance.

Unfortunately, Mallow didn't hear him. A cloud of sparkly purple pollen burst from Vileplume's top.

"Get away! Get away! Get away! GET AWAY!" Misty and Brock yelled at the top of their lungs, waving their arms. "It's poisonous!"

"Nooooo!" Mallow screeched. She scooped up Steenee and darted away as fast as her legs would carry her.

Sophocles was on a mission of his own. "Found it!" he declared, parting the leaves in a group of tall bushes. He had tracked down a Kanto Raichu!

Togedemaru seemed just as excited as Sophocles. The friendly little Pokémon rushed forward and raced circles around Raichu. It ran so fast that it created an electric charge that zapped Raichu! Raichu's head buzzed as it toppled over.

"Are you okay?" Sophocles asked, hurrying up to the fallen Raichu. Luckily, it was just stunned, and it seemed to be in a happy, drowsy state.

Lillie and Snowy had a much sweeter meeting with a new friend. "Snowy, that Pokémon is a Ninetales from Kanto," Lillie said.

Snowy slowly approached the regal Fox Pokémon. Ninetales gave the Alolan Vulpix a lick.

Lillie was a true student of all Pokémon, but she was especially interested in the Kanto region's evolved form of Vulpix. With its red eyes, the Fire-type Pokémon was truly mesmerizing.

"What a cute Pokémon!" Lana said when she and Popplio encountered a Dewgong. The Water- and Ice-type Pokémon was especially playful.

Pikachu and Ash were thrilled to see their friends from the Alola region enjoying the field trip so much.

"Coming to Kanto with everybody sure is fun!" Ash declared. "Hold on," he said, looking around. "Where did Rotom go?"

Of course, Rotom Dex was probably having the most fun of all. It was on a mission to catalog all Pokémon, everywhere, and the visit to Kanto presented so many opportunities to update data!

"If I keep this up, I'll be able to complete my data covering every Pokémon in Kanto!" Rotom Dex said.

"Now, check these out," Brock directed when the group was all back together. He and Misty each tossed a Poké Ball in the same direction.

"Notice any differences?" Brock asked when two Pokémon appeared.

Exeggutor from Kanto and Exeggutor from Alola were side by side. They seemed shocked to be standing next to each other, grumbling as they looked around.

The students from the Pokémon School were amazed. It was one thing to study the regional differences in Pokémon, but it was pretty awesome to compare the two side by side, right there on the grounds of Professor Oak's Pokémon laboratory.

"Kanto's Exeggutor is so short," Lana observed.

"I guess it doesn't get as much sun here," Kiawe commented.

"They're different, all right," Mallow said.

Alolan Exeggutor had a long, thick neck that swayed like a palm tree. Kanto Exeggutor's neck was so stubby, it was hard to see. But they both had three round heads, with sharp fangs and googly eyes. They both also had long tufts of grass that grew like hair.

"Here are my partners!" Brock said as he tossed two more Poké Balls. Two different Geodude appeared, both flexing their arm muscles.

Still, there were differences.

"That Geodude has no eyebrows," Lana pointed out.

"Are you saying those are eyebrows?" Sophocles asked.

Next, they compared a Muk from Alola to a Muk from Kanto.

"Muk, it's good to see you again . . ." Ash said, as his own Muk embraced him in a smelly, gunky hug.

"Last but not least . . ." Brock said, and a Kanto Marowak popped out of a Poké Ball.

"I present you with Alolan Marowak!" Kiawe said, throwing his own Poké Ball.

Immediately, the two Marowak butted heads and started spinning the bones each was carrying.

"Hey, cut it out!" Kiawe yelled.

"Come on, no fighting!" Brock scolded, but the two Marowak continued to face off. Brock and Kiawe had to hold them back.

"Their short-tempered personalities are the same," Mallow noted.

"Yeah, but I think their types are different," Sophocles said.

"You're right," Kiawe agreed. "My Marowak is a Fire- and Ghost-type."

"I know I read that the Kanto Marowak is a Ground-type," said Lillie.

"Right. I'm impressed!" said Brock.

Meanwhile, Pikachu was trying to separate the two Bone Keeper Pokémon, but they lashed out and sent Pikachu flying.

Next, Togedemaru tried to butt in, and soon it was a messy battle, with everyone chasing one another.

As soon as Pikachu was back on its feet, it stepped in. The Mouse Pokémon let out a massive, frustrated blast, sending an intense electric jolt through all the Pokémon and Trainers. Everyone was stunned!

CHAPTER 5

After they had all recovered from Pikachu's move, Lana realized something was wrong. "Popplio's missing!" she called out.

"Marowak's missing, too!" Kiawe said.

"They're GONE?!" Brock said in surprise.

Soon, all the Trainers had begun to search. Ash, Misty, and Brock looked together, walking along a wooded path.

"Popplio?" Ash called.

"Marowak?" yelled Brock.

"Where are you?" wondered Misty.

"Pika, pika?" Pikachu heard a rustling nearby.

Just then, a Caterpie wriggled out from behind a bush.

"You'd better stay away from me!" Misty shrieked, running to hide behind a tree.

Ash swallowed a laugh. "Some things stay the same," he said, shaking his head. "You're still scared of Bug-types?" he asked Misty.

"Bug-type Pokémon bug me more than I can say," Misty confessed, peeking out from behind the tree trunk.

"Misty, you sure haven't changed a bit," Ash said as they went back to searching.

"Brings back memories," Brock added. "I mean, of how the three of us used to travel together. We did lots of things and had lots of fun!"

"Although, not *everything* was fun," Misty replied thoughtfully.

"I enjoyed every moment of our journey," Ash told his friends.

"I'm a little jealous of how carefree you are," Misty told Ash. While Ash was still traveling the world on his Pokémon adventure, Misty had the big responsibility of being a Gym Leader.

Suddenly, they heard voices from deep among the trees. "What was that?" Ash cried.

"Let's see!" said Brock.

The friends crept into the forest. When they came to a clearing, they saw a group of Pokémon having a disagreement.

"It's Bulbasaur!" Ash cried with joy when he saw that his beloved Grass- and Poison-type Pokémon was among them.

"Bul-ba-saur!" The Seed Pokémon was overjoyed.

"How have you been doing?" Ash asked as Bulbasaur scampered over and bounded into his arms.

"Bul-ba-saur, saur, saur, saur," Bulbasaur replied, nuzzling up to Ash.

"Pika, pi!" Pikachu was happy to see its old buddy, too.

"It's been a long time," Brock said, watching the three cuddle. "Bulbasaur's thrilled!"

"Isn't it great?" Misty agreed.

After a while, Misty left Ash and Brock and ran to find Lana, Lillie, and Mallow. They were still looking for Popplio.

"Hey, guys!" Misty greeted them. "Still haven't found Popplio yet?"

"No," Lana replied, sounding bewildered. The others could hear the concern in her voice.

"There's a lake up ahead. I think we should check it out," Misty suggested. As always, she was upbeat and happy to lend a hand.

Misty led them to a bluff overlooking a clear blue lake.

"Maybe Popplio is playing in the water," Lana said hopefully, leaning down.

Just then, a Gyarados reared out of the water with a tremendous splash. The Atrocious Pokémon opened its mouth and let out a ferocious roar.

"Ahhhh!" Mallow, Lillie, and Misty cried. They took off running.

But Lana was not scared at all. "I'll take a look," she said, shedding her clothes to reveal a sleek blue swimsuit. She dove right in.

When Misty realized Lana had plunged in, she turned back around.

"Lana's brave," Misty said. "Well, she's not the only one who's brave! So I'm going to be brave, too!"

Misty dove into the water, and both Trainers swam deeper, searching for Popplio. They passed Poliwag, Magikarp, and other Water-type Pokémon.

It wasn't long before they found Popplio resting on the bottom of the lake with a Slowpoke and two Horsea.

Back on land, Ash and the others were still trying to track down Marowak.

"I know how Marowak gets. I sure hope it's not in a fight somewhere," Kiawe worried out loud.

"All right, then," Sophocles said, pulling a tiny gadget from his pocket. "I'll use this software I programmed—"

But as he spoke, the ground beneath him began to shake. With a loud rumble, Onix, the Rock Snake Pokémon, emerged from the craggy ground. It was gigantic, the size of a freight train!

"Let's do it, Turtonator!" Kiawe called out.

Kiawe had already thrown his Poké Ball when Brock held out his arms to stop him. "Just stay calm," Brock advised, his voice even. "As long as we do that, we'll be fine."

Ash, Sophocles, Kiawe, and their Pokémon held their breaths.

Onix quieted down and lowered its immense gray head to take a better look at the group. When it gave a gentle grunt and looked away, the Trainers all let out a sigh of relief.

Unfortunately, that was the same moment Marowak reappeared and threw its bone right in Onix's face.

"Marowak!" it yelled like a battle cry.

"I guess you wouldn't call that staying calm, right, Brock?" Kiawe admitted, holding back his frustration.

"You know what I'd say?" Brock replied. "Run!"

Everyone—Brock, Ash, Pikachu, Sophocles, Kiawe, Marowak, and Turtonator—took off at full speed!

Onix crashed and slithered behind them. It chased them deeper into the forest until they finally lost it—and found the rest of the Pokémon School group.

CHAPTER 6

"At least it's a big relief that we found everybody," said Ash as he looked around at the group. They were deep in the forest now. If Ash was right, they weren't very far from his house.

They had all met lots of friendly new Pokémon. Popplio and Marowak had gone missing. The girls had encountered a Gyarados, and the boys had a meeting with an Onix. It had been an eventful day!

But as soon as the whole gang was back together, a giant net swooped down, trapped all the Pokémon, and dragged them into the open hatch of a giant robot!

"What's that?!" Ash asked, instantly worried about Pikachu and the others. He looked at the

tall metal creature, which resembled . . .
Meowth!

Ash's answer came in the form of a battle
poem—Team Rocket style.

Prepare for trouble, like twerps used to do!
And make it double; we'll put a spell on you!
To protect the world from devastation!
To unite all people within our nation!
To denounce the evils of truth and love!
To extend our reach to the stars above!
Jessie!

James!

*Team Rocket, yours truly, blasts off at the
speed of light!*

*Surrender now or prepare yourselves for a
sentimental fight!*

Meowth, that's right!

Wobbuffet!

"Team Rocket!" Ash yelled. He realized that
Jessie, James, Meowth, and Wobbuffet must be
inside the giant robot—the robot that was
shaped like a giant, frightening Meowth!

Ash could hardly believe that the pesky
members of Team Rocket were in Kanto, too!
Then again, Team Rocket had a weird habit of
showing up wherever Ash and Pikachu
happened to be.

"By now, you'd think you would hang it up!"
Misty said, not at all surprised to run into their
old enemies.

"Give everyone's Pokémon back!" Brock
demanded.

"You may be an original twerp," Jessie told him from inside the robot, "but you're certainly not the best!"

"They're our Pokémon now," James added, "so give it a rest."

The robot lifted its steel foot and stomped down with a clank. The ground quaked.

"Some things never change," Ash said, knowing they'd have to battle. "Okay, Lycanroc, I choose you!"

At once, Lycanroc, the Wolf Pokémon, appeared.

"Use Rock Throw!" Ash directed, and Lycanroc sent a flurry of rocks flying.

"Rock my Robo-Meowth Mash!" Meowth replied, and an assault shot out from the Team Rocket robot's paw. The Pokémon School crew ducked for cover.

"Just like old times," Brock said, pulling out a Poké Ball. "Crobat, go!"

"Ready, steady . . . come on out!" Misty shouted, and Staryu appeared.

"Now, Lycanroc, Accelerock!" Ash cried.

Lycanroc sprang forward and hit the robot square in the chest.

"The NERVE!" Meowth cried, disgusted. "I'll teach you twerps a lesson!"

"Now, Crobat!" Brock directed. "Supersonic!"

Crobat focused its beam at the robot's paw just as Meowth was going to shoot another attack.

Meowth screeched in anger. "My paw won't work!" he cried. "What a jerk!"

Misty commanded Staryu to use Bubble Beam, and the Star Shape Pokémon shot a stream of bubbles at the robot—right where the net had dragged in all the kidnapped Pokémon! Staryu's beam kept pounding at the robot until the hatch popped open, and everyone's Pokémon burst out onto the forest floor.

"Pikachu!" Ash yelled happily as the Mouse Pokémon jumped into his arms.

The giant Meowth robot began to crackle and crumble, its circuits sparking. Even as the robot smashed to the ground, its mouth opened and Team Rocket appeared, unscathed.

"Didn't feel a thing," James declared, standing ready for another battle.

"Rise and shine, Mimikyu," Jessie demanded, throwing a Poké Ball.

But before she could tell Mimikyu how to attack, something fell from the sky above and landed in the forest clearing in a cloud of dust.

Ash recognized it at once. It was Bewear, the Strong Arm Pokémon from Alola. It was the same Bewear that had been hounding Team Rocket since they'd arrived in the tropical paradise. Now Bewear was in some kind of rocket, and it gathered Team Rocket in its strong arms and jetted up into the air.

"And it's liftoff with a new blast!" Team Rocket exclaimed with a sigh.

Ash, Misty, Brock, and their friends from the Pokémon School watched as Bewear and Team Rocket zoomed away.

"Anybody know what just happened?" Misty asked in disbelief.

"Don't look at me," Brock insisted.

Ash was about to explain, but then they all heard someone call out, "Ash!"

Ash would recognize that voice anywhere. It was his mom, Delia. He had missed her!

"Hey, Mom!" he called out, running toward her.

"Everything's all set for your welcome home party!" she assured him.

Ash knew his mother would throw a wonderful gathering for him and all his friends—new and old. Also, he realized that he was extremely hungry!

A little later, everyone was eating and talking and enjoying themselves.

"To reunions!" Professor Oak toasted.

"To reunions!" everyone responded.

"Welcome to Pallet Town, dears," Ash's mom said, looking around. "I hope you have time to see everything." She held Litten in her arms, and the Fire Cat Pokémon had never looked more content. It gave a happy purr.

"We will," Kiawe and Sophocles answered with certainty.

"If you want to see a complete mess, you should see Ash's room," Delia joked.

"Hey, Mom, stop it!" Ash begged, feeling embarrassed. He was happy when Rotom Dex flew by to distract everyone.

"What's the matter, Rotom?" Ash asked, seeing the device's frown. "Where have you been?"

"I can't find the last Pokémon to complete my Kanto Pokémon database," Rotom Dex complained. "Frustrating!" It had been busy all day, collecting information nonstop. How could it have missed one of Kanto's Pokémon?

While Alola had the allure of the many Island Guardians, Kanto had its own mysteries, too. Not far away, the Mythical Pokémon Mew watched the gathering at Ash's house. Mew, a Psychic-type Pokémon, had the ability to turn invisible to keep others from noticing it.

Mew floated away quietly into the deep woods, and Rotom would never even know that it had been so close.

After everyone had eaten and talked for a while, Professor Kukui stood up to thank their hostess. Ash's mom looked happy to have everyone there—especially Ash.

Professor Kukui wanted to talk about his lesson plan for the next day.

"Awesome!" Ash said, ready for anything. "What are we gonna do?"

"We're going to *Quick Attack* our way to battle at the Cerulean City Gym!" said Professor Kukui.

"Really?" Lana asked.

"At the Cerulean City Gym?" Mallow said, her voice filled with awe.

"Yup, that's right," Misty confirmed. "You are all going to battle at my Gym!"

"We're going to compete in a Gym battle . . ." Kiawe said to himself thoughtfully.

"I'm getting fired up!" Ash exclaimed. It had been a long time since he had been in a Gym battle, and what better place than Kanto to get back in the game!

CHAPTER 7

After a good night's rest, Ash woke up anxious. That day he would have a chance to compete in a Gym battle again—against Brock or Misty!

"Oh, YEAH!" Ash said as he and his friends rode toward the Cerulean City Gym.

The whole Pokémon School crew was in awe as they scrambled off the bus and walked toward the entrance. It was an enormous building with a glass roof that looked a lot like a cut diamond—a Gym that looked like a gem!

"Look!" Sophocles pointed out once they were inside. "Something's over there!"

There was "something" standing in the middle of the arena, not moving.

"Hey, it's Psyduck!" Ash said. Psyduck had

always been one of Misty's favorites, even if it was a little unpredictable.

"Pika, pika!" Of course Pikachu remembered Psyduck. Psyduck was unforgettable!

"So cute!" Lana said of the Water-type Pokémon.

"Hey!" Misty said, entering the arena. "Thanks a lot for minding the store, Psyduck!" She turned around and greeted her guests. "Welcome to Cerulean City Gym. My Gym!"

"Yeah! It's been so long since I've felt like this," Ash announced. "I want to get started battling right now!"

Professor Kukui stepped forward, not wanting Ash to get ahead of himself. "You all remember Misty and Brock," he said. "Misty is the leader of the Cerulean City Gym and an expert on Water-type Pokémon."

"Nice to see you all!" Misty said.

"And Brock is the former Pewter City Gym Leader and a Rock-type Pokémon expert," Professor Kukui declared.

"Hey there!" Brock said with a casual wave.

"These are the two you'll be battling! I want you all to feel the heat! It's like a Blast Burn!" said Professor Kukui.

Feel the heat? Ash thought that it was a funny line coming from Professor Kukui. After all, everyone knew that the Alola region was much hotter than Kanto.

Still, Ash had a good feeling about battling today. First of all, he had been right! Misty and Brock were the special guests that Principal Oak and Professor Kukui had talked about. Second of all, Ash knew Misty and Brock well. They would play fair and help the Pokémon School students learn about Gym battles, but they would also bring their best skills. It was going to be awesome!

"Pokémon Trainers in the Kanto region make their way from Gym to Gym while battling the Gym Leaders," Professor Kukui explained. "A Trainer who wins this battle receives a Gym badge as proof of victory."

Just hearing those words brought back so many memories for Ash. While he still had the same goal of becoming a Pokémon Master, a lot of other things had changed since his time in Kanto.

"The Cerulean City Gym has the Cascade Badge," Misty announced, holding up a badge that looked like a raindrop.

"And this is proof of victory at the Pewter City Gym," Brock said, holding out a shiny metal medallion. "The Boulder Badge!"

"Pretty, huh?" Lillie said. Lana agreed.

The Pokémon School students were all excited, but Ash knew the truth. His old friends were not just going to give those badges away. If the students wanted a Gym badge, they'd have to earn it.

"You won all the badges from the Kanto region, right?" Kiawe said to Ash.

"Sure did!" Ash replied. "You can win eight badges, and I won them all!"

Pikachu looked at Ash, uncertain.

"In my case, I gave him a badge out of pity," Misty told them with chuckle.

"Say, that story has a familiar ring," Brock added with a sly grin.

"What's going on?" Kiawe asked Ash. "What do they mean?"

Looking sheepish, Ash quickly changed the subject. "After you've collected all eight badges, you compete in the Pokémon League!"

"The Pokémon League?" Mallow repeated, interested.

"It's a big tournament where the best Trainers compete against one another!" Ash explained, making it sound very grand.

"Pika?" Pikachu gave Ash another questioning look.

"So why don't we start right off with some practice battles against Misty and Brock," Professor Kukui suggested. "Which of you lucky Trainers is up first?"

Everyone raised their hands at once and yelled, "Me!"

"I want to battle Misty!" Lana announced.

"Okay, you're in!" said Misty.

"Please?" begged Mallow. "One more?"

"I'd rather battle against Brock," Sophocles said.

"Me too," Kiawe agreed. With his Fire-type Pokémon, Kiawe assumed he'd have a better chance against a Trainer who specialized in Rock-type Pokémon.

"I wanna battle both of them!" Ash declared.

"Oh dear," Lillie said. "How do I choose?"

"Please don't worry," Misty said with a laugh. "It'll be fine.

"Now, ready to go?" Misty asked.

Lana and Mallow took their positions.

"Hey, guys!" Ash yelled. "Misty may not look it, but she's tough! Give it all you've got!"

"What do you mean by that, Ash? I look tough enough," Misty objected. "Okay, gang. Let's see what you can do!"

"I'll make sure to record all the action!" Rotom Dex promised, and everyone prepared to watch the first practice battle.

I'm all set to go!" Mallow declared. She looked to Lana to make sure she was also ready for their battle with Misty, the Cerulean City Gym Leader.

"All right, Steenee, Magical Leaf!" Mallow directed.

"Stee-nee, stee-nee!" The Fruit Pokémon created a vibrant green burst of glowing leaves that whooshed toward and twirled all around Psyduck.

"Popplio, use Bubble Beam!" Lana commanded. The Sea Lion Pokémon blasted tiny bubbles at Psyduck, bowling it over.

Psyduck lay on the arena ground, its webbed feet flailing in the air.

"All right!" Lana cheered.

"I think we won!" Mallow said with glee.

"Psyduck, use Water Gun!" Misty said, unfazed. A moment later, Psyduck was up and shooting a thick stream of water right at Popplio.

The Sea Lion Pokémon blew a bubble that gathered up all the water. The bubble grew and grew and grew. Popplio balanced it on its tiny pink nose like an oversized balloon.

"You're kidding!" Misty said, impressed.

"Popplio, that was great!" Lana told her battle partner.

"Popplio sucked in all the water!" Sophocles murmured, amazed.

"Lana, that was pretty creative!" Misty admitted. "So what do you do with it?"

"Balloon launch!" Lana called, and Popplio bounced the bubble in the air. Then, with a flip of its tail, it rolled the bubble at Psyduck. It rolled over Psyduck, trapping it inside. Then the bubble floated high in the air, taking Psyduck with it.

"When Lana and Popplio start their balloon work, they're simply amazing!" Mallow cheered.

"Yeah, they are. But you should know Psyduck is at its best when the chips are down," Misty told them. "Use Confusion!"

Psyduck grabbed its head and blinked again and again, trying to focus.

"Psyduck?" Misty said.

"Why isn't Psyduck using the move?" Rotom asked.

"Because Misty's Psyduck is kind of a flake," Ash told them.

"Use Magical Leaf one more time," Mallow said to Steenee.

"Stee-nee!" The glowing leaves hit the floating balloon head-on, and it burst. Psyduck fell straight down to the ground, landing on its head.

Mallow cringed when she saw Psyduck crash down. "Sorry about that!" she said.

"That's going to leave a mark," said Lana.

"Psyduck will be fine," Misty assured them. "No worries!"

Psyduck looked pained . . . and a little bewildered.

"Here it comes," warned Misty.

Pikachu watched, holding its breath.

All at once, Psyduck's expression changed. It grasped its head harder, shaking. Its eyes shot blue Confusion waves at Steenee and Popplio, stunning them and lifting them right up in the air.

"That's Confusion," Sophocles pointed out. "Why use that now?"

It didn't matter that the Confusion move had come late in the match. The attack had knocked Steenee and Popplio out of the battle.

"Yeah, that's enough," Misty called to Psyduck. "Great! I think it's time to let Steenee and Popplio down now."

"And that's that," Professor Kukui announced. "They're done."

"I always knew Misty and Psyduck made a great team!" Ash exclaimed.

"Thanks," Misty said, hugging the Duck Pokémon. "Psyduck is such a sweetheart." She stood up and faced her opponents. "You two have shown great battle instincts," Misty told Mallow and Lana with a smile.

"Oh, go on," Mallow responded, happy to get the compliment.

"I feel more confident already," Lana admitted.

"Now!" Brock called out to Lillie and Sophocles. "Time for our battle!"

"Geodude!" Brock's battle partner for the match was Geodude, the Rock Pokémon.

"Right! Togedemaru!" Sophocles shouted, raising his fist. "Zing Zap, let's go!"

Togedemaru lit up with an electrical charge and rolled right at Geodude. It made a solid hit on the Rock Pokémon, but Geodude just flexed its muscles and grinned.

"But how?" Sophocles questioned. "It didn't do a thing!"

"You're right," agreed Lillie.

"Why not?! Electric-type moves should have some effect! Geodude's a Rock- and Electric-type Pokémon!"

"But, I think you're talking about an Alolan Geodude," Brock said, looking a little smug. "The one from Kanto is a Rock- and Ground-type. Electric-type moves have no effect!"

Sophocles was annoyed with himself. How could he have forgotten about regional variants? It wasn't like him to miscalculate a matchup that way.

"Sophocles, you just leave everything to us," Lillie advised. "Snowy, Powder Snow!"

Snowy took a deep breath and sent a blast of Powder Snow to the other side of the arena.

"Geodude! Gyro Ball!" Brock yelled.

"Geo-dude!" The Rock Pokémon made fists and began to spin at great speed. When the Powder Snow hit, Geodude overwhelmed Snowy's move.

"Yeah! Awesome!" Ash cried.

"Dude." Geodude looked proud.

"But . . ." Sophocles stammered, confused. "Gyro Ball's an attack move, isn't it?"

"It can be used this way, as a defensive move, depending on how you train with it," Brock explained.

"I've never read about that," Lillie confessed. "Gym Leaders! They're the best!"

"Brock's no pushover," Sophocles said.

"I once had this challenger—during our battle, he taught me how to think outside the box," Brock told them.

Ash looked up when he heard that. He was pretty sure Brock was talking about him!

"I hope you all agree," Professor Kukui said, "Pokémon battling is amazing!"

The Pokémon School students all murmured with agreement. "With all the Pokémon types, moves, and training styles, the kinds of battles a Trainer can have are completely limitless," Professor Kukui went on.

"You also have to know your opponents' Pokémon well, so you can avoid the silly mistake I just made," Sophocles reminded everyone. Togedemaru and Sophocles laughed.

It was just a matter of time before they'd see whether Kiawe and Ash would also make silly mistakes in their big battles. Ash just knew that he wanted to battle well. He wanted to show his friends how much he had learned since he had left them and his hometown.

CHAPTER 9

So, Ash and Kiawe, you are next!" the professor said.

"Professor," Kiawe began, his fist clenched with determination. "I want a no-holds-barred Pokémon battle with Brock!"

"Me too," agreed Ash, "but with Misty!"

"You think you'll win?" Misty questioned. "That'll be the day."

"You may regret this, Kiawe," Brock said.

Professor Kukui had not planned on anyone having one-on-one battles, but Brock and Misty seemed game. Brock's battle with Kiawe would come first.

"I'll be the referee!" Misty volunteered. "This battle is one-on-one. The battle will be over when either side's Pokémon is unable to continue."

"I warn you," Kiawe said. "I'm confident about my strength."

"Happy to hear that!" Brock commended him. "What a Gym Leader looks for is how Trainer and Pokémon combine strengths! That's even more important than scoring a win."

"Which raises my confidence even more," Kiawe replied. He knew he and his Pokémon made a great team. "Turtonator, let's go!"

"Here's my partner. Come out!" Brock shouted, throwing his Poké Ball straight up.

Steelix burst from the ball with a grumbly growl.

"It's so big," Kiawe said in awe.

"It's Steelix!" Ash announced.

"Steelix. The Iron Snake Pokémon," Rotom shared. "A Steel- and Ground-type. Heat from deep underground strengthens its hide, and the pressure gives its body a toughness harder than metal."

"Let's see . . ." Sophocles began to strategize using one of his devices. "Steel-type Pokémon are weak against Fire-types, which means . . . Turtonator has the advantage."

"But wait," Lillie said. "Fire-type Pokémon are weak against Ground-type moves, so you could also say Steelix has the advantage."

"Then that means they're evenly matched!" Sophocles deduced.

"Brock! Kiawe! I wanna see a great battle out there!" Ash yelled to his friends.

"All right. Battle begin!" declared Misty.

"Turtonator, now! Use Flamethrower!" Turtonator shot a blast of flame from its snout.

"Steelix, use Gyro Ball!" Brock called out. He chuckled a little and said, "More thinking out of the box."

No one could believe it when Steelix's Gyro Ball dissolved Turtonator's flames, right before their eyes.

"All right, Steelix, Bind. Let's go!" cried Brock.

The Steel- and Ground-type Pokémon sprang forward and wrapped itself around Turtonator like a constricting snake!

"Turtonator, Shell Trap!" Kiawe shouted. With incredible force, Turtonator broke free, sending Steelix flying.

"Hey! Not bad!" Brock said.

"Not so bad yourself!" Kiawe responded.

The two opponents swapped moves, back and forth, both showing incredible strength.

After a while, Kiawe realized they needed to try something new. "We can't win this with a prolonged battle," he said to Turtonator, "so let's finish this off quickly with a Z-Move!"

The Z-Move was Kiawe's secret weapon. Only Trainers from the Alola region had earned the right to do Z-Moves.

"All right! From what I hear, Z-Moves make use of all your power!" said Brock. "Then we'll counter that with all *our* power! I'm not called Brock the Rock for nothing, you know!"

Ash could hardly contain his excitement. What did Brock have planned?

"Time for Mega Evolution!" Brock announced, pulling out a special pendant. When he held out the pendant, there was a flash of light, and Steelix began growing before their eyes.

Mega Steelix was much bigger, with a metal mane and gleaming crystal spikes. It roared.

Kiawe watched in awe. "Mega Evolution?" he murmured in disbelief.

"It's Mega Steelix!" Ash declared.

"Brand-new data!" Rotom Dex quickly began recording all the information.

"But how?" Mallow wondered. "Steelix got so much bigger!"

"That's amazing!" Lana agreed.

They were all curious about Mega Evolution, so Professor Kukui offered an explanation. "Mega Evolution is a phenomenon used in battle when a Pokémon's and its Trainer's hearts join as one. It's quite a remarkable thing to see."

"I've heard about Z-Moves," Brock said to Kiawe. "Show me one!"

"Right! And we'll win with it!" Kiawe said with certainty. "Turtonator, let's go!" Kiawe and Turtonator began a sequence of moves that they completed in unison. They looked like they were moving as one. "The zenith of my mind, body, and spirit! Become a raging fire and burn!" Turtonator grunted with effort. "Inferno Overdrive!" Kiawe commanded.

Turtonator shook with effort as it built a mighty blast of fire. It heaved the flames at Steelix in one fluid motion.

Brock assumed a shielding stance, and Mega Steelix stood confident.

"What happened?" Kiawe asked after the move was finished.

"How could Mega Steelix withstand a Z-Move?" Ash questioned. All the Pokémon School students were stunned.

"That Z-Move had an incredible amount of power!" Brock said to Kiawe. "It definitely affected Mega Steelix! But Turtonator wasn't able to go that one last step!" Then Brock declared Mega Steelix's final move. "Use Stone Edge!"

With a mighty grunt, Steelix set off a series of crystal spikes that tunneled underground and then shot out of the arena floor. They erupted in a line aimed right at Turtonator.

"Turtonator! Use Dragon Tail!" Kiawe directed at the last second, but it was too little too late. "Turtonator!" he called out.

"Turtonator is unable to battle!" Misty announced. "So Steelix wins!"

"Kiawe lost!" Mallow said, not believing it.

"And all that after Kiawe and Turtonator worked so hard," said Lillie.

"Gym Leaders *are* strong," Lana pointed out.

"This data will never *EVER* be deleted!" Rotom claimed, still hyped up from the battle.

"What was that?" Sophocles asked, looking out at the arena. Something had happened to Steelix.

"After a battle, Mega-Evolved Pokémon return to normal," Professor Kukui explained.

"That was great work, Steelix!" Brock said, pulling out his Poké Ball. "Thanks!"

"Turtonator, you okay?" Kiawe asked, patting the Blast Turtle Pokémon on the head. It was a sweet moment . . . until Marowak came by and whacked them both with its bone.

"Maro, maro, wak-wak-wak!" Marowak was not happy about the loss.

"Marowak!" Brock scolded. "I know how frustrating losing can be, but you should praise them for their work!"

"Maro." The Bone Keeper Pokémon still wanted to pout more.

"What did you think?" Professor Kukui asked his students. "Tell me."

"I loved it! I was on the edge of my seat!" Lillie confessed.

Everyone agreed with Lillie. They all thought Pokémon Gym battles were the best!

"Misty, I'm next, don't forget!" Ash said.

"Who, me?" Misty asked. "Forget? Never! You're next! Promise!"

The whole Pokémon School crew held their breaths. Ash against his old traveling companion and the Cerulean City Gym Leader, Misty—this was going to be good!

CHAPTER 10

As Misty was taking her place for her battle with Ash, she pushed a button on a remote control. At once, the Gym arena began to change.

"Whoa," Ash murmured. The floor of the arena sunk into the ground and filled to make a deep pool of water. "That's so awesome!" Ash exclaimed. "A Water-type Pokémon battlefield! When you say Cerulean City Gym, it's gotta be water!"

"The field changes with whatever Pokémon are battling on it!" Misty said with a laugh and a hint of warning in her voice.

Kiawe wasn't sure why Ash was so excited. "Does Ash realize that he's just been put at a disadvantage?" he asked Sophocles.

"Where is his Pokémon supposed to stand?" Sophocles wondered.

"I got this covered!" Ash assured his friends. "Pikachu, you're up!" Without a pause, Pikachu leaped out to the rock bridge that ran around the edge of the pool.

"I figured it would be Pikachu!" Misty said.

"Yeah! You know us," Ash admitted.

"Since Misty uses Water-type Pokémon, an Electric-type like Pikachu has the advantage!" Rotom announced to everyone.

"Misty versus Ash! The rules remain the same," Brock declared. "One-on-one!"

"Now the *other* internationally known beauty!" Misty announced. "Go, my one and only!" She threw her Poké Ball up with a twirl, and a giant Pokémon sprang out with a deafening roar. Pikachu shuddered.

"It's Gyarados!" Ash yelled.

"Yes, Gyarados, the Atrocious Pokémon," Rotom confirmed. "A Water- and Flying-type. Rumors exist of a town that made Gyarados

angry. That town was burned to the ground in
one night, leaving no trace!"

Rotom quivered as it told the story, but Brock
was not fazed. "Gyarados versus Pikachu!" he
said. "Begin!"

"Pikachu! Use Thunderbolt!" Ash directed,
and Pikachu instantly geared up and shot a bolt
toward Gyarados.

"All right, Hydro Pump!" said Misty, and
Gyarados's water stream met Pikachu's bolt in
the middle, canceling it out.

"See that? Water-type moves *can* stop Electric-type Pokémon," Misty commented.

"Does not compute!" insisted Rotom. "Does not compute!"

Ash wasn't going to give up that easily. He knew Pikachu wouldn't either. "Use Quick Attack!" he cried.

Pikachu made a direct hit in the Atrocious Pokémon's face, knocking it over. But Gyarados was too strong to stay down for long.

"Rain Dance," commanded Misty. "GO!" Gyarados reared up to its full height, and a cloud formed around its head. The cloud darkened and grew until it filled the arena, and then it started to rain.

"But—how can it rain in here?" Mallow wondered out loud.

"It feels so good," said Lana.

"Don't worry, Pikachu!" Ash said to his partner. Pikachu went ahead and started building up an Electro Ball.

"Gyarados, use Hurricane!" Misty called.

Just as Pikachu shot Electro Ball across the
arena with a fierce swat of its tail, Gyarados
used Hurricane to knock the attack off target
with a gust of damaging wind. Pikachu went
spinning to the ground.

"That sure packed a lot of power!" Kiawe noted.

"How about that, Ash? There's nowhere for
you to run," Misty chided.

"Using Hurricane in the rain was a good
move for Misty! It even canceled out that
Electric-type move that could've caused
damage," Professor Kukui said. "So *that's*
Misty's plan to defeat Pikachu."

"Pikachu, are you okay?" Ash asked.

"Pika!" Pikachu was still in battle mode.

"Feast your eyes, Ash!" Misty said, flashing a piece of jewelry that was looped around her ponytail. It took Ash a moment to realize it was a pendant—like Brock's. "Looks great on me, don't you think?"

"You've got one, too?!" Ash said with a gulp. Misty had the pendant to help Gyarados evolve to be even more ferocious?

"Strong, valiant, and powerful!" Misty twirled as she spoke in a dramatic voice. "Now, my beautiful blue sweetheart! Mega Evolve!"

Gyarados roared as it transformed, its fins growing longer, its body growing thicker, and its expression turning nastier. Mega Gyarados meant business.

"Hey, Misty, this is fun!" Ash yelled to his friend. Pikachu was just as determined.

"Sure is!" Misty agreed. "Now use Hydro Pump!"

Mega Gyarados used Hydro Pump, and it sent a tidal-wave-sized blast of water at Pikachu. It knocked the Mouse Pokémon into the pool.

"You're not getting away!" Misty called out to Pikachu. "Use Crunch!"

Mega Gyarados dove into the water with a splash.

Pikachu swam to the edge and began to run across the land bridge. Gyarados was right behind, smashing into the bridge, crumbling it to pieces. "Pikachu, use Iron Tail!" Ash cried.

"It won't work from that posture," Sophocles commented as Pikachu kept running.

"Now jump on Gyarados!" Ash shouted. "Quick, use Iron Tail!"

"Pika, pika, pika, pika." Pikachu bounded onto Mega Gyarados's back. The Mouse Pokémon panted as it ran with all its might, nearing the other Pokémon's monstrous head. Once there, Pikachu used Iron Tail.

"Look at that!" Mallow cheered. "A direct hit!"

Mega Gyarados collapsed in the water, but Ash knew the battle wasn't over.

"You two always *were* good!" Misty said.

"Here it comes! One more time!" Ash said to his battle partner.

"Hurricane, go!" Misty shouted, and Mega Gyarados rose from the water, conjuring a rainy cyclone that spiraled toward the ceiling. It picked up Pikachu, and the Mouse Pokémon disappeared in the gusty cloud.

"Use Thunderbolt," Ash directed. Pikachu sent the charge through the spinning cloud, but nothing happened.

"That's a Rain Dance and Hurricane

combination! Not a single challenger in my Gym has ever broken through it!" Misty bragged.

"That was nice of you to let me know," Ash replied, feeling more confident. "Thanks, Misty! Breaking through stuff like that is what makes battling awesome!"

"What are you talking about?" Misty questioned.

"Hey, Pikachu!" Ash cried. "Can you hear me?"

"Pika, pika!" the little yellow Pokémon replied.

"Climb up the Hurricane!" he yelled.

"Does not compute! Does not compute!" Rotom Dex repeated.

But Ash was surer than he'd ever been. If Pikachu couldn't break through the Hurricane, the Mouse Pokémon would need another way out. "Use Quick Attack and then climb up the electricity!" Ash directed.

"Electric platforms!" Professor Kukui yelled when he figured out what Ash had planned.

They all watched the intense, spinning cloud and waited. At long last, Pikachu shot out the top.

"It worked!" Kiawe and Sophocles cried, both amazed.

"Uh-huh," Brock said. "That's Ash for you."

"I think it's time for a Z-Move! Let's go, Pikachu!" Ash called out.

"Pika!" Ash's battle partner was ready and willing.

Ash and Pikachu began their Z-Move sequence, gaining flow and power.

"All right, here we go with FULL POWER, NOW!" Ash called out. "Use Gigavolt Havoc!"

Pikachu focused all its power. It crackled with energy and threw a massive electric pulse right at Mega Gyarados.

The Atrocious Pokémon dropped into the pool.

"Gyarados is unable to battle! Pikachu is the winner!" Brock announced.

"Way to go! You did it, buddy!" Ash was so proud of the way he and Pikachu had battled!

"That was an amazing battle, Gyarados!" Misty said to her battle partner as she held up the Poké Ball. She turned to her opponents. "I think you've gotten a bit stronger, Ash."

Ash appreciated the compliment, especially coming from Misty. "I've gotta agree with you," he replied.

"But that little kid inside of you still stays just the same," Misty added.

"Little kid inside of me?!" Ash repeated, trying to figure out what Misty meant.

"We're talking *really* little," Misty continued.

"Now, now," Brock said, bringing the teasing to an end.

"Wasn't that amazing?" Mallow said.

"Yes!" Lillie answered at once. She was really fired up by the whole Gym battle scene.

"Misty's skill with Water-type Pokémon is so inspiring!" Lana added with admiration.

"I'm sure this battle conjured up all kinds of emotions!" Professor Kukui said to his students. "Treasure this experience, and when you're back in Alola, keep it with you!"

"Here," Misty said, handing replica badges to the students she had battled. "They're not real, but they'll remind you of today."

"This is so great," Mallow said, examining the design on the badge. "Thanks a lot!"

"Cerulean is the color of water!" Lana noted. "A beautiful blue!"

Brock had given his opponents keepsake badges, too.

"I never would guess that it's a fake," Sophocles said.

"I'll win a real battle next time we meet," Kiawe said with confidence. After his battle with Brock, he looked more ready than ever to devote himself to training.

"You're welcome to try," Brock replied. Even

though he was now studying to be a Pokémon doctor, he had not lost his battling abilities from his days of being the Pewter City Gym Leader!

"Misty, do you mind if we come back again?" Lana asked.

"Any time!" Misty said, feeling glad that everyone had had such a good experience at her Gym.

"I just had a great idea," Professor Kukui said. "I'd like to add the Pokémon League as part of Alola's great traditions."

"I think that's a marvelous idea," Professor Oak said.

"And some badges would fit the bill-*Lillipup*!" Principal Oak agreed, adding another Pokémon pun for good measure.

"That was a lot of fun," Brock said.

"It really felt like old times," added Misty.

"Now it's your turn to come visit me in Alola!" Ash said to his former traveling companions.

"Count on it, Ash!" Misty and Brock answered together.

"I will!" Ash really meant it. It would be hard

to say good-bye to his old pals if he didn't believe he would see them again soon. He had almost forgotten how much he, Misty, and Brock had shared. That time had been so early on in his own adventure, and he had come so far.

He really loved learning at the Pokémon School. He felt like he grew in his Pokémon knowledge every day. But the time he spent with Misty and Brock was when it all began for him. It was the foundation for everything he knew and loved about Pokémon. He would never forget that time, and he would never forget them. They would always be part of his journey to become the best Pokémon Master he could be!